W9-AQL-932

Mummies, Masks, & Mourners

by Margaret Berrill

illustrated by Chris Molan
and with photographs

Lodestar Books   E. P. Dutton   New York

Originally published in Great Britain in 1989 by
Hamish Hamilton Children's Books

First published in the United States in 1990 by
E. P. Dutton, New York, New York,
a division of Penguin Books USA Inc.

Conceived, designed and produced by
Belitha Press Ltd
31 Newington Green, London N16 9PU
Copyright © in this format Belitha Press Ltd 1989
Creative Director: Treld Bicknell
Designer: Gillian Riley
Editor: Felicity Trotman
Picture Researcher: Ambreen Husain

The author and publishers wish to thank the following for
permission to reproduce copyright material:
The MacQuitty International Collection, title page (clay
figure), pp 5, 33, 34 *top*
Reproduced by Courtesy of the Trustees of the British
Museum, title page (mummy), pp 5 *bottom*, 16 *right*, 25, 26,
31, 43 *both*, 44 *both*
The State Hermitage Museum, Leningrad, title page
(cockerel motif), pp 22, 23, 24 *both*
The Mansell Collection, pp 4, 12
The University Museum of National Antiquities, Oslo, pp 6
top left, 38, 39, 40 *both*
The Greenland Museum, pp 6 *center left*, 41, 42 *both*
Xinhua News Agency, pp 6 *bottom right*, 28, 29 *inset*
The Ancient Art and Architecture Collection, p 7 *top*
Werner Forman Archive, p 7 *bottom*
Ministry of Tourism and Culture, Ankara, p 8
By Courtesy of the Archaeology and Anthropology
Department, Cambridge University, p 11 *both*

Library of Congress Cataloging-in-Publication Data

Berrill, Margaret
    Mummies, masks, and mourners / by Margaret
Berrill; illustrated by Chris Molan and with
photographs.
        p.   cm.
    Includes index.
    Summary: Discusses funeral rites practiced in the
past in different parts of the world and how through
archeologists we have come to know about them.
    ISBN 0-525-67282-6
    1. Funeral rites and ceremonies—History—
Juvenile literature.   2. Burial customs—History
—Juvenile literature.   3. Funeral rites and
ceremonies, Ancient—Juvenile literature.   [1.
Funeral rites and ceremonies—History.   2.
Burial customs—History.]   I. Molan, Chris, ill.
II. Title.
GT3150.B44   1990   89-31822
393′.9—dc20   CIP
                                                 AC

Map and diagram by Gillian Riley

Printed in Hong Kong for Imago Publishing
First American Edition COBE 10 9 8 7 6 5 4 3 2 1

Robert Harding Picture Library, pp 13, 21 *bottom*, 46
Bridgeman Art Library, pp 16 *left*, 19 *left*
Uni-Dia-Verlag, p 19 *top right*
Museum of Fine Arts, Boston, p 19 *bottom right*
British School of Archaeology in Iraq, p 21 *both top*
Society for Anglo-Chinese Understanding, p 29 *main picture*
Fototeca Unione, p 30 *top*
Museo Archeologico di L'Aquila, p 30 *bottom*
Courtesy Department of Library Services, American
Museum of Natural History, p 34 *bottom* (photo by E. H. Morris)
Detroit Institute of Arts, pp 35, 36 *bottom* (photos by Dirk
Bakker)
City Art Museum of St Louis, p 36 *top*
from *The Mound Builders*, copyright 1928, renewed 1956 by
H. C. Shetrone, published by D. Appleton and Co, 1928,
reproduced in *The First American* by C. W. Ceram,
published by Harcourt Brace Jovanovich, 1971, p 37
London Borough of Camden Local History Library, p 45 *top*
John Gay, p 45 *bottom*

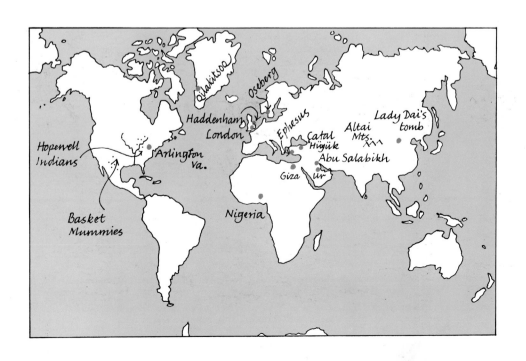

Contents

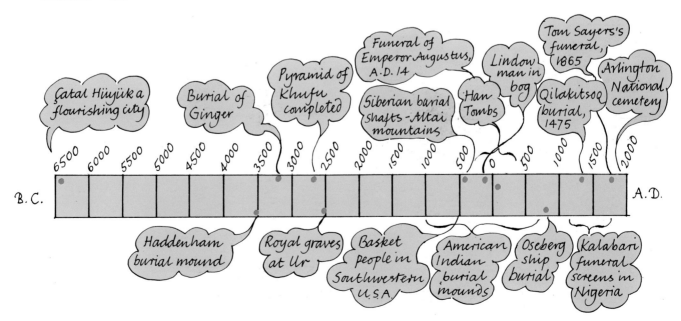

"Bring out your dead!" The cry followed the clanging of the plague bell. Families struggled to heave dead bodies onto a cart as it moved slowly along the dark street. People died from the plague week after week in that terrible year of 1664. In the worst week, the infectious disease killed 7,000 Londoners. The bodies were carted away and dumped in huge pits outside London. The city's graveyards were crammed.

Nowadays these plague pits lie beneath the roads and buildings of the modern city. Trains rumble over the plague pit that lies under the mainline station at Liverpool Street in east London. But if such a burial ground was discovered by chance, it would be obvious that something terrible had happened in the past.

Like all living things, people's bodies begin to rot away and smell when they die. It is not healthy or pleasant for dead bodies to rot near living people. So all over the world and as far back in time as we know, different peoples have had to deal with their dead. Most often bodies

These prints, made in the year of the great plague, show various death scenes—several people dying of the disease in a sickroom where a coffin stands waiting; dead bodies being collected; open graves; and coffins being carried to burial.

Pottery models of acrobats buried in a Chinese tomb about 2,000 years ago

This Egyptian mummy of a boy is from the Roman period, about the second century A.D. Only wealthy people could afford such elaborate bandaging.

have been cremated or buried in the ground. But other peoples have allowed birds or animals to eat the flesh, or sent bodies out to sea on boats. The ancient Egyptians used special methods to try to stop bodies from rotting. Only in disasters like wars or plagues have dead bodies been simply dumped together or left unburied.

Peoples everywhere also shared certain feelings and beliefs about the dead, which have led to special customs called funeral rites.

First, they have wanted to show the importance of the person who died, whether to family and friends, to tribe or town, or even to the entire country. To show that a funeral was a special occasion, clothes, music, and food were all chosen according to strict rules. Ancient Egyptians wore pale blue clothes; later, Europeans and Americans wore black; and in the Far East white is still the color of mourning. Nowadays funerals are more simple, and friends and relatives are expected to recover quickly or to hide their grief, although their sad feelings are quite natural and can last for years.

A wooden chair from the Oseberg ship burial

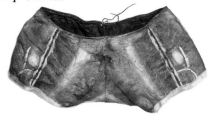

Shorts made from sealskin, worn by one of the mummies found in Qilakitsoq, in Greenland

Many peoples believed that an invisible part of the dead person, called the spirit, would go on to another life, where it might need the same things as in this life. So women were often buried with their cooking pots or hair combs, men with their work tools, and children with their toys.

Graves are like time capsules. Experts called archeologists can find out about the way people lived in the past by digging up things that are buried in the earth. The remains of buildings, pots, jewelry, weapons, tools—even tiny specks of pollen or pieces of grain—can give them information.

Archeologists call objects that are buried with the dead "grave goods." The grave goods of rich people were great treasures. Food, drink, and

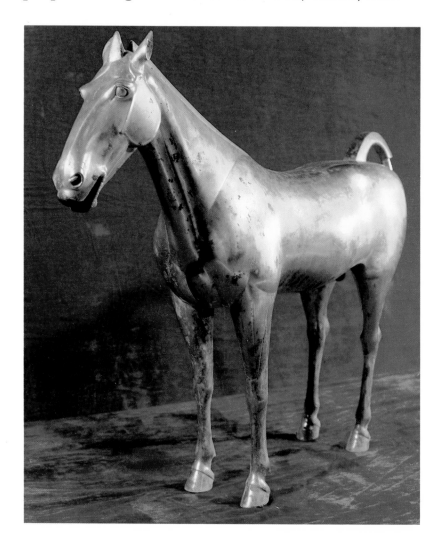

This gilded bronze horse is from the tomb of an emperor of the Han Dynasty.

Women mourners painted on the wall of an Egyptian tomb

transport were often provided for the dead. Servants were sometimes killed and buried with their masters. Then people came to believe that models of servants could be buried instead. In China today, paper models of people and houses are still carried in funeral processions and then burned.

As well as looking after the spirit of the dead person, many peoples also feared that the spirit might come back and harm the living, so they went to great trouble to keep it away. Sometimes a special hole was cut in the wall of the house and then sealed up after the dead body was carried out, so the spirit would not be able to find the door. People thought that if the body was carried out headfirst the spirit would see the way and return later. Coffins are still carried out of houses feetfirst.

In this book you can read about some of the funeral rites that were practiced in different parts of the world, and how we know about them.

Clay figures from a Han tomb

2 Çatal Hüyük

Part of a wall painting in a house in Çatal Hüyük

The archeologist James Mellaart spent many years making maps of the mounds that are landmarks in the flat plain of central Turkey. These mounds were built up long ago, over hundreds of years, as people made new buildings on top of the remains of older ones.

As soon as he looked at the mound of Çatal Hüyük, James Mellaart knew that it was very special. People of the late Stone Age, who used polished stone tools and weapons, had lived there about 8,500 years ago. No later buildings had been made on their remains.

Çatal Hüyük is a prehistoric town. Everything we know about it has been pieced together by archeologists from the remains they have found. Five or six thousand people lived there in one-story houses. There were no outside doors, and ladders were needed to climb onto the houses so that it was easy to keep enemies out. There were no streets and people walked along on top of the houses, climbing in through a hole in the roof and then down a ladder into the main room, which had benches and sleeping platforms built into the walls.

The people at Çatal Hüyük seem to have been very religious, for many of the rooms are shrines where they worshiped. However, only a small part of the town has been excavated so far. Does the rest of Çatal Hüyük include so many shrines, or are most of them in this one area? Time and further excavations may tell.

Many small statuettes and figurines of a goddess have been found. Sometimes she is a girl, sometimes a mother, and sometimes an old woman. The people also worshiped a god whose sacred animal was a bull. Plaster heads of bulls with real horns decorate the walls of the shrines.

Wall paintings show vultures eating the flesh from dead bodies. Some of the vultures have human legs, and some of the bodies have no heads. Skulls were particularly important, and they have been found in baskets beneath the bulls' heads in the shrines.

Working from the evidence of bones and wall paintings, archeologists think that the people of Çatal Hüyük used air burials, leaving the bodies in the open air so that birds and animals could pick the bones clean. Dead bodies were probably left outside the town for vultures to eat the flesh. Afterward the bones were collected and placed in the shrines or houses. The people of Çatal Hüyük seem to have slept on their sleeping platforms with the bones of their ancestors buried under them! The priestesses who carried out the rituals in the shrines may even have been dressed as vultures.

East Anglia is a very flat region, with rich, peaty soil. One field may cover several acres. This land is good for growing wheat. But strangely, around 1980 a big hump appeared in a completely flat wheat field at Haddenham near Ely.

Peat is made very slowly by plants such as moss and reeds that rot away and sink into water. As new plants grow on top, the bottom layers are pressed down and become hard. At Haddenham modern farming methods of plowing and draining water from the land had caused the level of the topsoil to sink down, too, and so the hump was revealed after being hidden for hundreds of years. Archeologists identified it as a long barrow, or burial mound, from the late Stone Age, when people were settling in villages, growing crops, and using polished stone tools.

In 1986, archeologists from Cambridge University began to excavate the mound. When

A reconstruction of the wooden burial chamber found at Haddenham

A pile of the neatly sorted bones found inside the burial chamber

they had dug down through three feet (one meter) of topsoil, they realized that they had made a unique find. Many Stone Age burial mounds have been excavated, and experts have always suspected that they once contained wooden burial chambers, but in every mound excavated the chamber had rotted away. Here at Haddenham was a big roof of blackened oak planks.

The wood had been preserved by the wet peat for over 5,000 years. It was like a large wooden box twenty-six feet (eight meters) long and six feet (two meters) wide, making it the oldest complete wooden building ever discovered in Britain. Water and chemicals were sprayed over it constantly, for it was very fragile and would crumble to dust when touched.

The people seem to have been good carpenters and used an adz to shape the planks of the burial chamber, which were then fixed together with pegs and held up by posts.

What would the archeologists find inside the box? When they took the lid off, just as they expected, there were neatly sorted bones. This suggested that the people who lived there in 3500 B.C. had used air burials to dispose of their dead.

FACT BOX

Haddenham is in Cambridgeshire, part of the region of East Anglia in eastern England.

The dig was led by Ian Hodder.

When peat and water are found together, the land is called a bog. Peat is used for fuel and fertilizer.

FACT BOX

Giza is near Cairo on the Nile River.

Egyptian civilization grew up along the Nile, which flooded each year, producing fertile land where plentiful crops could grow. Beyond this there was desert.

There were three great ages in Egypt's history:
1. the Old Kingdom (about 2686–2181 B.C.), when the pharaohs built their pyramids
2. the Middle Kingdom (about 2133–1633 B.C.), when Egypt was settled and prosperous
3. the New Kingdom (about 1567–1084 B.C.), when Egypt ruled other lands, and the pharaohs built great temples and were buried in the Valley of the Kings

Sir Flinders Petrie worked in Egypt for forty-six years.

The Pyramid of Khufu took twenty years to build. It was completed about 2600 B.C. About 100,000 men worked on it.

In 1880, the archeologist Sir Flinders Petrie arrived at the pyramids of Giza. His Egyptian helpers were astonished when he chose to set up camp with an oil lamp and stove in a disused *mastaba*. At night he worked stark naked inside the hot pyramids, then spent hours writing up notes in his stuffy, smoky *mastaba*. By day he worked in a pink vest and pants, which, he said, frightened away the tourists who constantly interrupted his work.

Tourists had been visiting the three great stone pyramids at Giza since the time of the Greeks and Romans, 2,000 years earlier. Guarded by the Sphinx, the pyramids had stood at the edge of the desert, buffeted by sandstorms, for 4,500 years. Everyone knew that they were the tombs of the pharaohs, and that their contents had been stolen in ancient times.

Sir Flinders Petrie

Was there anything else to be discovered? Excavations are still going on at Giza. The three great pyramids each had two temples, one by the river and one near the pyramid, linked by a causeway. There are also the remains of smaller pyramids with temples, streets of tombs made for high officials and private citizens, and altars and statues of gods and kings. These things have been preserved by the hot, dry Egyptian climate. Many are still to be excavated in this city of the dead.

The Great Pyramid of Khufu (Cheops)

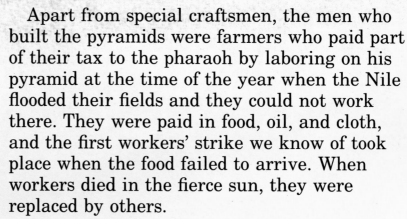

Apart from special craftsmen, the men who built the pyramids were farmers who paid part of their tax to the pharaoh by laboring on his pyramid at the time of the year when the Nile flooded their fields and they could not work there. They were paid in food, oil, and cloth, and the first workers' strike we know of took place when the food failed to arrive. When workers died in the fierce sun, they were replaced by others.

Over two million stone blocks, each weighing more than two modern cars, were used to build the Great Pyramid of Khufu (Cheops). There were no bulldozers or cranes, not even wheeled carts to help move the massive stones.

The building of solid stone, apart from the burial chamber and a few passages, is so big that if it were hollow both St. Paul's Cathedral and the Houses of Parliament in London, or the Capitol and the Pentagon in Washington, D.C., would fit inside it.

After the pharaoh's funeral, passages were blocked with rubble and closed with stone doors. There were concealed entrances, dead-end passages, and false doors—all to prevent people from disturbing the dead. But in spite of these precautions, the lure of riches encouraged robbers to break in and steal.

5 Making Mummies

From the earliest times, the Egyptians buried their dead in simple graves in the desert. In the British Museum there is a body, nicknamed Ginger because of the color of his hair, which was wrapped in skins or matting and buried with some knives and pots more than 5,000 years ago. Ginger's body was dried out and preserved by contact with hot sand. There is another body like Ginger's in the American Museum of Natural History. Poor people continued to be buried like this, but from at least 2600 B.C. the Egyptians began to prepare some bodies as mummies.

When a wealthy Egyptian died, the body was brought by boat to the embalmers' workshop. The complete treatment took seventy days, though the less well-off could choose between two cheaper treatments. First the brain and the soft parts inside the body were removed and preserved in jars. The body was then covered with natron, a salt that dried out all the moisture. After about forty days, the body was washed and embalmed. Jewelry was put on the body—one king wore twenty-two bangles and twenty-seven rings. Sometimes the face was made up and clothes were put on. At every stage there were ritual gestures from priests and embalmers.

The coffin of a priestess called Shepermut, decorated with the figures of gods, including Anubis, the god of embalming, identified by his jackal head. Shepermut herself is shown kneeling, on the chest. The picture above right shows the mummy known as Ginger.

Bandaging took fifteen days, beginning with fingers and toes, which were wrapped one by one. As many as 410 yards (375 meters) of linen were used in bandages and shrouds for one mummy. Between each layer, hot oils were poured over to stiffen the wrappings. Magical jewels, such as scarabs, were placed among the bandages. Sometimes careless embalmers included dead flies, lizards, or a dead mouse.

The mummy was placed in one or more painted wooden coffins. Over the bandages the mummy wore a mask showing his face with a long wig and collar. Later the mask was extended to form a figure-hugging decorated coffin, to make the dead person look like Osiris, the god of the underworld. Sometimes there were several coffins, one inside another. A stone sarcophagus was used as an outer container for pharaohs and the wealthy.

Despite all these efforts, many expensively prepared mummies did not last as well as Ginger. The jewels wrapped with the mummies, and goods placed in the tomb, were a great temptation to robbers.

FACT BOX

A mummy is a body that has been preserved for a long time after death, whether deliberately or through natural conditions.

Mummy comes from the Arabic word for bitumen or pitch, the tar we use to surface roads. Travelers who saw badly prepared, blackened bodies thought that they had been dipped in pitch.

Archeologists have found many mummies of cats, dogs, crocodiles, and other animals. The Egyptians thought their gods could appear on earth as animals.

Some underground tombs contain four million ibis mummies stacked up in pottery jars.

6 In the Field of Reeds

When the mummy was ready, a funeral procession accompanied it to the tomb. Why did the Egyptians bury their dead in this way? They believed that people could live again after death.

First, priests performed the ceremony of the Opening of the Mouth, so that the dead person's *ka,* or soul, could reenter the body and give it the power to eat, breathe, and move. The *ka* would be able to recognize its body by the mask it wore. If the dead person had been good, he could then enjoy the afterlife in the Field of Reeds. After the ceremony, the mummy was placed in its coffin or sarcophagus and the tomb was sealed up.

To help people reach the Field of Reeds, the priests put together a collection of spells and answers to questions the soul might be asked, called the *Book of the Dead.* A copy was placed in each tomb.

In the Field of Reeds, life went on just as it did on earth, so it was important that the dead person had with him everything that he might need—clothes, furniture, makeup, games, and amusements, and especially food. Real food was included in the tomb—the Pharaoh Tutankhamen had 116 baskets of fruit, 40 jars of wine, boxes of roast duck, and loaves and cakes with him.

In case this failed, the walls were painted with magic spells and scenes of daily life. These paintings tell us a great deal about Egyptian life. Land had to be plowed and crops sowed and harvested just as on earth, so little figures called *ushabtis* were placed in the tombs.

A rich person might have 365 mummy-shaped *ushabtis*, one to work on each day of the year, and 36 overseers with whips to make sure that they did not slack.

A wall painting from a tomb, showing food for the dead

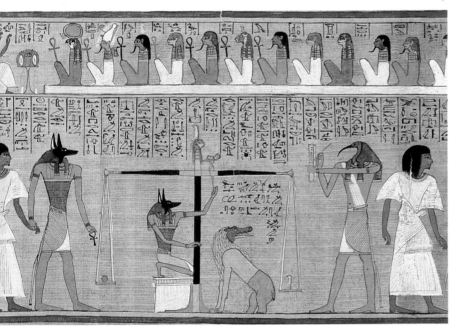

People believed that the dead were ferried across a river for a ceremony called the Weighing of the Heart. This picture from the Book of the Dead shows the god of the dead, Osiris, and other gods, watching as a dead person's heart is weighed. If the heart was heavy with sin and weighed more than the ostrich feather, which represented truth and goodness, the monster Ammit would gobble it up. Ammit was part crocodile, part hippopotamus, and part lion. But even a wicked person was safe if a heart scarab was placed in the mummy wrappings.

The expertly bandaged mummy of Nesmutaatneru

19

FACT BOX

The Sumerians were the first people we know about who lived in Sumer, a land on the Tigris and Euphrates rivers. They arrived there some time before 3000 B.C., and their language died out in 2000 B.C. The land is now South Iraq.

Abu Salabikh is about ninety-five miles (one hundred and fifty kilometers) south of modern Baghdad. American and British excavations took place there between the 1960's and the 1980's. The dig was led by Nicholas Postgate.

Why do we count our time in hours of sixty minutes? Why do our weeks have seven days? These questions lead us back thousands of years to the Sumerians, who counted in units of sixty as well as units of ten, and worshipped seven planets. Much of our knowledge comes from the work of the archeologist Leonard Woolley, who excavated the Sumerian city of Ur. He found a large cemetery, including royal graves made about 2500 B.C. A king and queen had been buried with many treasures and also with seventy-four servants, who seem to have taken poison.

Royal graves are not the only ones to be found. Recent excavations in the Sumerian town of Abu Salabikh aimed to discover more about the way ordinary people lived. A large family and servants probably lived in one big house that they excavated. It seems to have belonged to an official who dealt with land and its owners. Clay tablets found there refer to areas of land belonging to the king, and even to the policeman.

Above, the skeletons of two onagers found in a grave at Abu Salabikh. Left, archeologists digging out the western end of the grave under the house at Abu Salabikh.

A detail from the Standard of Ur, a decorated box found in the royal graves. No one knows what it was used for, but it may have been a musical instrument. One side of the box shows battle scenes. This side shows the victory feast that followed. Captives and onagers are being paraded before the king.

The house was built around an open courtyard. It was rebuilt several times, and the latest rebuilding was about the same date as the royal graves were made at Ur. At this later date, the dead of the family were buried under the rooms of the house in six brick-lined tombs. But an earlier burial was also found in a huge hole under the central courtyard.

At one end of the pit, some jewelry of copper, silver, and semiprecious stones was found, though most of the rest of the grave had been robbed not long after the burial. At the other end, the archeologists found the remains of two onagers. The chariot or cart they were to pull had rotted away. Imagine carrying about sixty-five and a half cubic yards (fifty cubic meters) of earth from the inner courtyard out through the house, to make a hole which then had to be filled in again. It would be like burying your family car underneath one of the rooms of your house!

This elegant carriage, which was found in one of the tombs, probably came to the Altai from China. It cannot have been used much on the rocky, frozen ground, but it is shown here carrying the coffins of a chieftain and his woman to burial. The horses are wearing masks with antlers.

Deep in the remote Altai Mountains of Siberia lies the Pazyryk Valley. Russian archeologists working in the high, flat, dry valley earlier this century had to use an unusual method when they excavated the deep burial shafts beneath five huge cairns of stone. The shafts had become frozen during the long, harsh winters and, insulated from summer warmth by the stone mounds, had remained frozen for more than 2,000 years. The archeologists had to pour on thousands of buckets of hot water to melt the ground where gravel was set in ice, as hard as concrete.

Just as we freeze food today to preserve it, the ice had preserved objects made of materials like wool, cloth, and leather, which would normally have rotted away long ago. There was the oldest carpet ever discovered, which had come from Persia (now Iran), and silks from China older than any found in that country.

Over a fifty-year period around the fifth century B.C., tribes living in the Altai Mountains had dug shafts thirteen to twenty-three feet (four to seven meters) deep in unfrozen ground to bury their chieftains. They placed a low chamber of larch logs at the bottom of each shaft. Wooden mallets, stakes, shovels, and trolleys used for the work were found in the tombs. The larch chambers were lined with felt and covered with layers of birch bark, branches of shrubs, and felt. After the burial each shaft was filled with layers of logs and stones. On top was piled the earth from the shaft, then stones dragged to the site on sleds pulled by men on horseback. Inside each burial chamber the archeologists found a coffin hollowed out of the trunk of a huge larch tree.

Some were decorated with carvings or cut-out figures of cockerels, others with deer or tigers. In each coffin lay the bodies of a tall, strong man and a woman killed to be his companion in the afterlife. The bodies had been preserved by embalming, possibly in salt. One chieftain probably died in battle, as he had been scalped. His skull was stuffed with larch cones, pine needles, and soil. His skin was so well preserved that complicated tattoos of real and imaginary animals could be clearly seen.

Not long after the burials, grave robbers plundered all of the tombs. Archeologists think they stole many precious objects of gold, silver, and copper, for these metals can be mined nearby. They left behind things that were of no value to them but that tell a great deal about the daily life of the Altai tribesmen. The finds agree with Greek and Chinese writings about mysterious and far-off tribes.

The mourners had provided for their dead chieftains clothes of fur, felt, and linen; leather pouches and bags; small collapsible tables for serving meat; wooden pillows; carpets and wall hangings from Persia; silks and mirrors from China; drums and harps; and weapons.

Below, is the skin of the right arm of the tattooed chieftain. The intricate design includes six animals between wrist and shoulder. Below the slit at the top right, you can see the twisted-round body of a deer with an eagle's beak and very long antlers, which end in birds' heads. These also run along its neck and the tip of its tail. The tattooing was probably done by pricking the skin and rubbing in soot. The tattoos would have looked blue during life. They were either a sign of manhood or showed that the chieftain was of noble birth.

A stuffed felt swan. There was one at each corner of a canopy that decorated the Chinese carriage.

Everything the Altai used was beautifully decorated, often with cutouts of animals. Shapes were cut from leather or brightly colored felt, and stamped with gold leaf or tin foil. This scene of a lion pouncing on a goat was appliquéd in felt on a saddle cover.

But most important of all, the robbers had left untouched the bodies of horses, in one tomb as many as sixteen, which had been buried outside the larch chamber in the shaft under the logs and stones. With them was all their equipment—saddles, bridles, saddle cloths, and even fantastic headdresses and masks for special occasions.

The Altai tribesmen were on horseback all day long. A chieftain might own thousands of horses as well as his personal riding horses, which were killed and buried with him when he died. The tribesmen did not have money. Instead, everything was valued in horses. A horse might be worth as much as a man's life. Horses provided meat, milk, and skins as well as transport, and were traded with neighbors like the Chinese who needed them for warfare. Other animals were much less important. Crops were probably not grown at all, since no grain or grinding equipment has been found in the tombs. The tribes of the Altai seem to have shared much of their way of life with nomads who lived in tents and wagons covered with felt or birch bark. They moved about with their herds across the huge, flat grasslands of Europe and Asia. But the Altai themselves probably lived most of the year in timber huts, which they copied in their burial chambers.

9 Lindow Man

In the summer of 1984, two men were busy at their job of cutting peat from a bog at Lindow Moss in Cheshire. As they worked they noticed something strange. It was part of a man's body. The police thought that the man had been murdered and his body put in the bog, but they did not have to find the murderer, because scientists soon discovered that the man had been dead for several thousand years. His body had been left in a pool and preserved by chemicals in the water. Gradually the peat had formed all around it. Who was he, and how long had he been there?

Archeologists could not say when he had died, because no pots or tools were buried with him. But many other experts set about their own detective work, finding out all they could about Lindow Man. He also has a nickname: Pete Marsh!

The body of Lindow Man, slightly squashed by the weight of peat which lay on it for hundreds of years

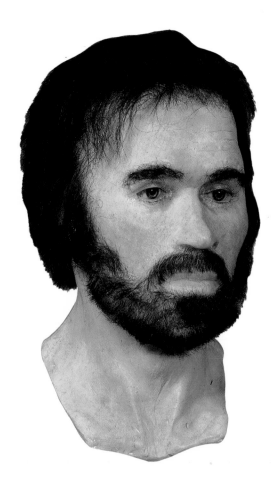

By studying the layers of peat in which he was found, scientists could tell that he had died over 2,000 years before. He was a strong, healthy man, about twenty-five years old, with dark hair and a beard. His fingernails were well cared for, so he was not used to working hard with his hands. He was wearing no clothes, except for a band of fox fur around his arm. For his last meal he ate some flat bread, made without yeast, and part of the crust was burned. He had been hit on the head, strangled, and his throat had been cut.

Why had he been killed like this? So far there is no definite answer to this question. Perhaps the Celtic people of Lindow thought that their god would be pleased if they killed someone as a gift or sacrifice. They may even have decided to kill the person unlucky enough to receive the burnt crust. Perhaps he had been cowardly in battle or shirked hard work. The Roman writer Tacitus tells us that among the Celtic tribes being pressed down in a bog was the punishment for such people.

A modern model showing how Lindow Man may have looked, based on the evidence of all the experts who examined his body. A powerful microscope even showed that his beard had been trimmed with scissors, which were very rare. This suggests that he may have been an important person.

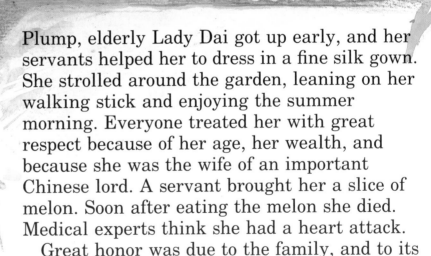

Plump, elderly Lady Dai got up early, and her servants helped her to dress in a fine silk gown. She strolled around the garden, leaning on her walking stick and enjoying the summer morning. Everyone treated her with great respect because of her age, her wealth, and because she was the wife of an important Chinese lord. A servant brought her a slice of melon. Soon after eating the melon she died. Medical experts think she had a heart attack.

Great honor was due to the family, and to its ancestors who had died in the past. Their spirits had power over the living and their advice was asked on all important matters. Lady Dai was carefully buried at the bottom of a deep shaft covered by a mound of earth. There she lay undisturbed for over 2,100 years.

Then, in 1972, there were plans to build a hospital outside the Chinese city of Changsha. A mound over twenty-one yards (twenty meters) high and covered with trees lay in the path of the bulldozers. Archeologists were

One of a set of lacquer bowls for holding wine from Lady Dai's tomb. Lacquerware cost ten times as much as bronze. It was made by applying coat after coat of resin from a special tree to wooden or bamboo objects. A hard, shiny surface was built up. Painted with designs, lacquerware objects were colorful and hard-wearing but delicate and lightweight.

This cut-away painting shows Lady Dai's body, wrapped in silk, inside a nest of coffins, surrounded by compartments containing burial goods, all enclosed in a huge wooden box.

called in to investigate. Under the mound, at the bottom of a shaft over seventeen yards (sixteen meters) deep and filled with earth, they found a huge wooden box. It contained the four coffins of Lady Dai. Her body was wrapped in twenty layers of silk. Her coffins were covered with many layers of bamboo matting, a layer of charcoal weighing almost five tons (five metric tons), and a layer of white clay almost one yard (one meter) thick. These materials had preserved Lady Dai's body.

The goods in the grave were very well preserved too. There were clothes for warm and cold weather, mostly of silk—silk shoes, stockings, and embroidered mitts—all neatly folded in bamboo cases. There were the remains of a huge selection of food: cereals made into cakes with honey; vegetables; fruit including plums, pears, and strawberries; animals including pigs, cows, and sheep; and many kinds of fish. There were model servants and a model orchestra, and many beautiful objects of pottery, bronze, and lacquerware. All were

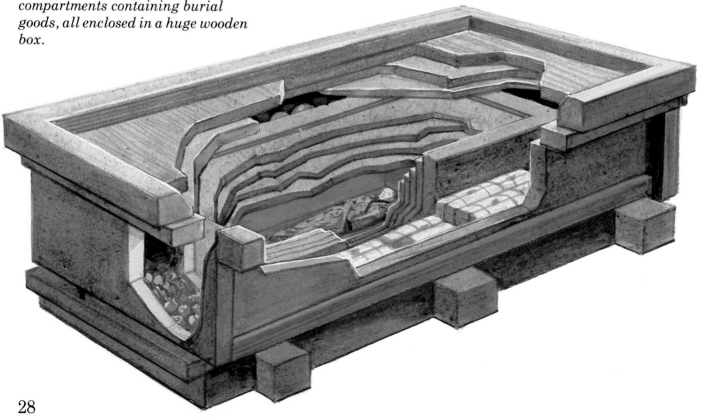

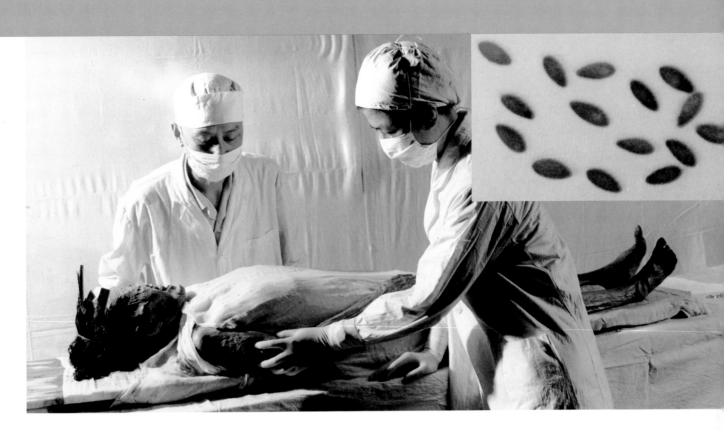

listed on strips of bamboo tied in bundles. This was Lady Dai's *Send-off Book*—and 2,100 years later archeologists found it very useful for checking the grave goods.

Lady Dai's tomb is not the only one that we know about from the Han period—in fact many thousands of graves have been found. They were made for all sorts of people, from princes to prisoners.

Many princes and high officials were buried in mound-covered tombs. We know from writings that these great mounds were built by workers who had committed crimes or become bankrupt. As prisoners, their punishment was to build roads and palaces, and do other heavy work for the emperor. In 1972, not far from the tomb of one of the Han emperors, archeologists excavated a prisoner-workers' graveyard. There were over 10,000 graves. Here the archeologists found no luxury goods. Instead, many of the skeletons in the empty graves wore iron shackles around their necks and ankles. Weighed down by their chains, they had carried earth for the emperor's burial mound.

Medical experts examining the mummy of Lady Dai, who was about 50 years old. Herbal medicines, still used to treat heart disease, were found in the grave. In her stomach 138 seeds from the last melon she ate were found (inset).

FACT BOX

The Han emperors ruled China from about 200 B.C. to A.D. 200. Han rulers were the first to govern the whole country, and this brought peace and success after years of war and rebellions.

In the Han emperors' workshops, craftsmen produced many beautiful goods like those found in Lady Dai's tomb. They made objects of bronze, pottery, porcelain (very fine china), silk, and lacquerware.

The prisoner-worker graves are located at Xianyang City in Shaanxi province, China.

Above, the mausoleum of Augustus in Rome. Below, Roman funeral processions were held at night. This marble carving shows a dead person lying on a special funeral bed carried by eight men. The canopy over the bed is decorated with a moon and stars. The procession is led by musicians playing horns and pipes, followed by men weeping and beating their breasts. Behind the funeral bed, women mourners cling to one another. The smaller figures may be hired women mourners.

In 1868, John Turtle Wood, a British engineer and architect, was excavating at Ephesus, hoping to find the temple of the Greek goddess Artemis. Two years later he did discover it, and on the way he found remains of burial grounds from the Roman Empire.

Leading from one of the city gates were two roads. For nearly two miles (three kilometers) along one road, Wood found the huge tombs of important officials. Carved on them were their names, descriptions of their life, and rank. Beside the other road, he found many tombs of white marble, marking the graves of humbler people. Along the mountainside above the road, there was a way for pedestrians, and in natural folds in the rock, the Romans had made arched tombs called *columbaria*. They had little holes for urns and chests containing the ashes of ordinary people.

Nearly all Romans were cremated, and their tombs were placed outside their cities, for health reasons. Only a few very powerful Romans, like the first emperor, Augustus, were given permission by the ruling senate to build a tomb within the city walls. Before he died, in A.D. 14, Augustus wrote an account of all his achievements, which he listed on bronze plates nailed to the walls of his mausoleum. It was

there to impress people and remind them of the power of the emperor.

Because tombs were outside the city, important Romans used funeral processions to make sure that people did not forget the part their ancestors had played in the history of Rome. When someone died, a mask was made of his face, which was displayed in the family home. At family funerals, the masks of all the family ancestors were worn by actors, dressed in the correct clothes, who rode in chariots in the funeral procession. There might also be hired mourners, music, a banquet, and funeral sports. There was a funeral speech that included gaps for weeping and wailing, and the audience joined in like a chorus. All this cost a great deal of money—one funeral cost enough to support 800 ordinary families for a year!

But even less wealthy people could hope to be remembered if travelers stopped to look at their tomb. Sometimes the messages spoke directly to passersby: "I pray you read it willingly, and read it again; don't let it bore you, my friend."

The sarcophagus of a Roman boy, Aemilius Daphnus, showing a scene of boys playing a game with nuts. Perhaps he had enjoyed playing such a game himself. In Roman times a wealthy man might leave instructions in his will for nuts to be given to the poor children of his town.

FACT BOX

The Roman Empire grew up between 227 B.C. and A.D. 106.

At its most powerful it stretched from Hadrian's Wall, in the north of England, to the Persian Gulf.

Ephesus was a Greek city in Lydia, now western Turkey. Later it became a Roman port.

"I want to dig for buried treasure, and explore among the Indians, and paint pictures, and wear a gun, and go to college." Ann Axtell Morris wrote these words in her diary nearly a hundred years ago. She was only six, but grew up to do almost all these things. She worked with her husband, Earl Morris, to make many important discoveries about the Indian peoples of the United States.

Earl Morris excavated an area of the southwestern United States that is called the Four Corners because it is the only place where four states—Utah, Colorado, New Mexico, and Arizona—meet. In northeastern Arizona, now the Canyon de Chelly National Monument, the Morrises' finds included graves containing the skeletons and mummies of Indian peoples who had lived there up to 2,000 years earlier. Although finds of mummies were rare, some bodies had been preserved in the hot, dry climate.

Because of their great skill in weaving baskets, these Indians are now known as the Basket Makers. Storage baskets up to 100 inches (250 centimeters) around have been found. Baskets were not used simply for carrying goods. They were used for burials and even for cooking. The baskets could not be heated over fire, of course, so they were made watertight with resin, and filled with water. Then the food to be cooked, and red-hot stones, were lowered into the water. The Basket Makers grew maize, squash, and later, beans. They hunted using an *atlatl*, or throwing stick, and from about 500–700, bows and arrows.

Earlier Basket people lived in caves and pithouses. They dumped rubbish outside their houses, and here graves have been found. Sometimes bodies were buried carefully wrapped in furs and skins, with grave goods like weapons and ornaments. This suggests that their owners believed in a life after death. The Morrises found many graves. One contained only skulls, and another contained bodies, but the two did not belong together. There was the riddle of a grave containing "shoes without feet, necklaces without a neck, and a pipe without a mouth." This was how Ann Morris described a grave containing a pair of arms and hands,

FACT BOX

Earl Morris was born in 1889, and died in 1956. He dug up his first pot and skeleton when he was three years old!

Many of the Morrises' finds can be seen in the University of Colorado Museum.

lying on a bed of clean grass. The hands were wearing two pairs of beautifully woven sandals patterned in black and red. There were three shell necklaces, a basketful of beads, and a stone pipe. Had the person died in a landslide, with only his arms available for burial?

In a huge basket the Morrises found four children, apparently unharmed. On top of them were fourteen more babies and children. Perhaps they died from an infectious disease.

It seems that the Morrises often took the bodies for granted, as when they used a long box containing a well-preserved mummy as their breakfast table at the site of their excavations! But Ann Morris also describes a find of well-preserved flutes buried with a mummy. Few flutes have been found in good condition, and Earl Morris could not resist trying out a tune. As the flute "lived" again in its music, Ann Morris says that they half expected the old flute player to rise from his grave. But of course he did not; instead, they were suddenly very aware of the hundreds of years that stretched back to the time when he had been alive, like them, standing there.

Earl Morris, left, with some of his finds in Canyon del Muerte (Death Canyon). There are 22 skulls, baskets, and vases. The shapeless bundles are mummies wrapped in woven mats. The mummy second from the right is very well preserved. Some of the canyons where the Morrises excavated are so deep and narrow that the sun only shines there for four hours a day. After dark, every sound seems louder, and the atmosphere can encourage thoughts of ghosts and haunting.

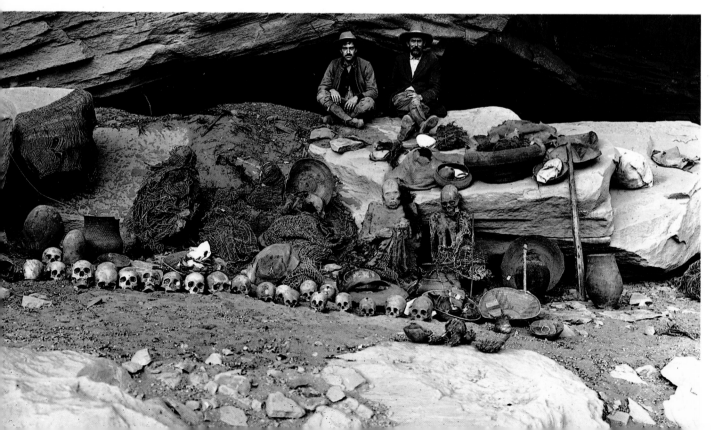

When the American archeologist Henry Clyde Shetrone began excavating the Seip burial mound of the Hopewell Indians in Ross County, Ohio, in 1926, he did not expect to be buried himself. He dug a trench into the mound making a wall thirty-three feet (ten meters) high. Suddenly the great wall of earth began to sway and toppled down on him. Fortunately, his helpers rushed to the rescue. He seemed to be dead, but he soon came to and was taken to a hospital to have his broken bones set.

There are over 100,000 mounds in the United States, dating back as far as 1000 B.C. Some are well preserved, and some have been flattened by plowing. Others have been vandalized by grave robbers. Most are in the valleys of the Mississippi and Ohio rivers.

A Hopewell pipe in the form of a beaver with pearl eyes. The tobacco was loaded into a bowl in the beaver's back, and the smoke was breathed in through the small hole.

35

Above, a painting made around 1850 showing an excavation into a mound in the Mississippi Valley. Below, a larger than life-size hand, made of mica, found in a Hopewell Indian grave.

The mound Shetrone was excavating contained ninety-nine skeletons in different layers, including four adults and two children in a burial chamber made of logs. Was this the tomb of a chieftain's family? It contained rich objects of tortoiseshell, silver, and copper, including a copper axe weighing almost twenty-eight pounds (thirteen kilograms). This would have been used for important ceremonies. But what led the newspapers to describe the mound as "the great pearl burial" were thousands and thousands of river pearls, worth several million dollars today.

From excavations, archeologists have been able to work out how the Hopewell Indians dealt with their dead. After the site for a mound was chosen, the trees and topsoil were cleared. Next the area was plastered with clay, slightly below ground level, and covered with a layer of sand or gravel. Then a large wooden building was put up. If it was too big to have a roof, smaller buildings for cremations and burials were made inside the main wall. The bodies of most of the people who died were first stripped of flesh, then cremated in special clay-lined pits, or placed in containers made of logs on platforms near the pits. Chiefs and those of high rank were not cremated. Their bodies were laid out in log tombs, on low clay platforms, surrounded by grave goods. These were broken or "killed," so that their spirits could go with the dead to the afterlife.

The archeologists found the teeth and claws of grizzly bears from the Rocky Mountains; shells and alligator and shark teeth from the Gulf of Mexico; copper from Lake Superior; and mica from the Carolinas. All these things, as well as the river pearls found by the bucketful in some graves, were used to make the earrings, necklaces, and bracelets that the Hopewell men and women had worn as adornments in life and that were buried with them when they died.

What music, dancing, wailing, or chanting of special words took place at Hopewell funerals? What afterlife did they believe in? There are no written records, and grave goods cannot tell us the answers. We can only use our imaginations.

FACT BOX

Up till about 700 the Adena Indians, then the Hopewells, built burial mounds in the northern Mississippi Valley. The Seip mound was built sometime before 500.

The people got their name because more than thirty mounds were found on land belonging to a Captain Hopewell.

From around 700 to 1700, other peoples built much larger mounds farther south, from St. Louis to the Gulf of Mexico. They are shaped like flat-topped pyramids, and had wooden temples on top that have rotted away. Some were built up in layers—as many as twelve—and they were used for worship, not burial. Graveyards have been found nearby.

The largest mound is Canokia Mound in Illinois. Its base area is nearly 200,000 square feet (18,600 square meters) and is larger than that of Khufu (Cheops), the biggest Egyptian pyramid. The equivalent of 20,000 truckloads of earth was used to build one mound, but for tools the builders had only their hands, baskets, and sacks made of animal hide.

The grave of a Hopewell man and woman from a mound in Ohio. The Hopewell Indians loved ornaments. Both skeletons wear copper bracelets, and the man has a copper plate above his skull. Between his feet there is a copper axe. Some Hopewell skeletons have been found wearing copper noses!

14 Viking Ship Burials

Wooden utensils found in the Oseberg ship

Saturday, August 8, was the birthday of the Norwegian archeologist Gabriel Gustavson, and on that day in 1903 he received a marvelous present—the first news of Norway's greatest archeological discovery. Farm workers had dug into a mound of peat almost twenty feet (six meters) high and one hundred and thirty feet (forty meters) wide at Oseberg. They thought they had found a Viking ship. Gustavson concluded that they were probably right, for other buried ships had been found in the area.

Gustavson had celebrated another birthday before his team finished excavating the Oseberg ship. It had been well preserved by the clay surrounding it beneath the mound of peat. The weight of the mound had damaged it slightly, but worse damage had been done by grave robbers, who had tunneled into the wooden grave chamber at the stern of the boat and disturbed the remains of a young woman.

This young woman may have been the Viking queen Asa. Attended by an old woman, she was lying in the burial chamber among beds, pillows, blankets, and eiderdowns. It seemed

FACT BOX

Oseberg is about forty-five miles (seventy-two kilometers) south of Norway's capital, Oslo, on the Oslo Fjord.

The excavations continued from 1903–1904.

The ship and its treasures are now in the Archeological Museum, University of Oslo.

Ship burials containing the remains of important people have been found by the sea in Norway, Sweden, Denmark, and also England. Queen Asa died between A.D. 800 and 900.

The richest ship burial ever found was at Sutton Hoo in England.

Gabriel Gustavson, standing third from left, and his team with the ship at Oseberg. This was one of the first excavations where photographs were taken regularly as a record of the work.

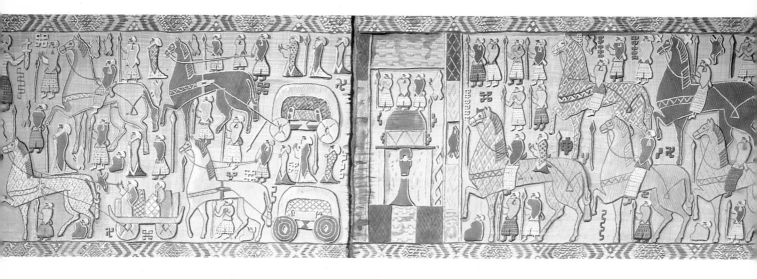

An unusual find was this splendid tapestry with pictures of battles and horses, carts, wagons, and warriors with shields and spears. The tapestry was probably hung on the walls of the grave chamber. Other tapestries as old as this have rotted away, but this one survived in the dry air of the burial chamber.

Like the ship itself, and sleds found with it, this wagon is beautifully carved.

that the robbers had stolen her jewelry, as one of the chests and barrels with her had been broken open and was empty. But many other wonderful things remained in the ship.

In the bows were wooden sleds and a four-wheeled wagon, beautifully carved like the ship itself. There were tents, beds, a chair, and weaving equipment. There were oars, a gangplank, and other equipment belonging to the boat, as well as homely utensils like a knife, wooden plates and jugs, and iron cauldrons.

The mourners had provided the young queen with food at her burial. A large ox was laid out on two wooden planks. There were walnuts, hazelnuts, wheat, cress, and a barrel of apples.

Why did the Vikings bury people in ships?

The sea played a most important part in the lives of the Vikings, and they sailed great distances. Perhaps ship burial was chosen to show that they were masters of the sea. Or was the ship simply the largest of the grave goods? It was probably another example of people believing that the dead made a journey to the afterlife.

15 The Mummies of Qilakitsoq

This is the view from the spot on the west coast of Greenland where the mummies were found.

Two brothers, from the modern town of Ummanaq on the west coast of Greenland, were out hunting one day in 1972. Near the old, abandoned Inuit settlement of Qilakitsoq, they noticed a strange arrangement of stones on the ground. Lifting some of them, they discovered several well-preserved bodies.

For five years no one took any notice of their find. Then the director of the Greenland Museum realized from their photographs that they had made a unique discovery. Experts gave the date of the burial as 1475.

In two graves, the bodies of six women and two children had been buried one on top of the other, with animal skins in between. The bodies were lying under an overhanging rock where they were protected from sun, snow, and rain. The bottom of each grave was lined with skins and grass. Gradually the very low temperature had freeze-dried the bodies into mummies.

The Inuit people believed that if they were lucky they would reach heaven, where they would be happy hunting the plentiful game. But in hell, the land of the gloomy, they would find nothing to eat except butterflies.

FACT BOX

Greenland, capital Nuuk, is a very large island between Iceland and Canada. Qilakitsoq is on the west coast.

The Inuit are Eskimo people. They live in Greenland, Canada, and Alaska.

The mummies from Qilakitsoq are now on display in the Greenland Museum, Nuuk.

41

This young woman, one of six found at Qilakitsoq, was well dressed for her long journey to the Land of the Dead. All the mummies wore heavy pants, jackets, and boots stuffed with grass to keep in the warmth. The skins of seals, caribou, polar bears, and birds were used in their clothing.

The body of a tiny boy was the most well-preserved of the mummies—so well, in fact, that he looked more like a doll than a human child.

After they had carefully examined the bodies, scientists, medical experts, and archeologists were left with many questions.

Why were the bodies all buried together, and were they buried at the same time? Other graves at Qilakitsoq had contained only one person, and were nearer to the settlement. Perhaps they belonged to one family. Two of the women may have been sisters, for their faces were tattooed with the same pattern. The tattoos also showed that they were married and lived in the same settlement. The children may have been set out to die in the cold, if their mother had already died. This custom may seem terribly cruel, but food was very scarce and the children might have died slowly of starvation if there was no one to look after them.

Did they all die together? Could they have drowned when their skin canoe capsized? This does not seem likely, as there were no remains of a boat in the grave. It would have been buried with them, being considered too unlucky for anyone else to use.

They may have starved to death, but the bodies seemed well fed, and there were still traces of food in one—including head lice, which the Inuit enjoyed eating! Perhaps they died from eating bad meat that had been kept too long.

So far there are no answers to these questions. Perhaps science will find a way to answer them in the future.

Percy Amaury Talbot, the man sent by the British early in this century to help govern the Kalabari part of Nigeria in West Africa, was a very severe person. Someone said that if a lizard should walk into his wife's room while she was bathing, Talbot would put that lizard in jail! So when Garrick Braide began causing trouble for the British around 1914, everyone expected him to be harshly dealt with. He was put in prison for a while. Braide was a local preacher who became very powerful.

Braide urged people to give up their faith in African gods, and to burn the carved wooden funeral screens called foreheads of the dead. The people believed that every plant, object, and person had its own spirit. In humans, the spirit was found in the forehead.

For hundreds of years, the Kalabari people lived in fishing villages among the creeks, islands, and swamps of the great delta of the Niger River. Traveling in canoes up to sixty-five feet (twenty meters) long and rowed by as many as twenty oarsmen, they traded their fish with inland people up the river. They were warlike and often raided each others' villages.

But from the time five hundred years ago when explorers and traders from Europe first arrived on the coast of West Africa, the Kalabari became important links in the trading process. They sold ivory and slaves from inland to the European traders, in return for goods like guns, alcohol, and brassware. They also began to see books and pictures.

Gradually the Kalabari built up great trading households made up of groups of canoes, used for trading but also armed with cannons. They kept in touch with one another by drum signals. A house chief led his group of canoes in time of war when the king might need his help. In return, the house chief took part in governing the people.

Wooden model of an ancestor

A Kalabari chief with his supporters and slaves around 1880. European hats were worn to show high status.

FACT BOX

The Kalabari are people who live in the delta of the Niger River, in Nigeria, West Africa.

Their screens are called, in the Ijaw language, *Nduen Fobara*—which means "foreheads of the dead."

Some of the screens can be seen in the Museum of Mankind, London.

A funeral screen. The initials of the trading house (BB) can be seen on the left-hand side. The chief wears the mask which he wore in the masked dances. The small heads represent slaves and supporters, or captives taken in war. Sometimes screens show trading items like cannon balls or mirrors.

Detail from a funeral screen

After the chief of a powerful trading house died, a wooden sculpture or funeral screen was made, to honor him as an ancestor and as a house for his spirit. It was placed in a dimly lit shrine in their main meeting house. The new head of the house had to make offerings of food and drink and keep a fire always burning before the screen. People saw the screens as dangerous and powerful images of their ancestors, which could do them good or harm.

These were the funeral screens that Garrick Braide the preacher wanted to destroy, but some of them survived and are still important to the Kalabari today. Garrick Braide himself is said to have died when his boat was struck by lightning, but the church he founded still survives. Fortunately Percy Talbot was very interested in the Kalabari way of life. He saved some funeral screens and gave them to museums, where experts are still studying them.

44

17 A London Funeral Procession

The funeral procession of Tom Sayers took three hours to pass the crowd of 100,000 Londoners who had come to line the route from Camden Town up the steep hill to Highgate Cemetery. Sayers was the last great bare-fisted fighter. He had fought thirty-seven rounds without boxing gloves against an American to a draw in the world championships.

His funeral procession in 1865 was a great spectacle, with carriages drawn by black horses wearing black ostrich plumes. The mourners were dressed in black from head to toe, the ladies wearing black veils and black jet jewelry. But at Tom Sayers' funeral, the sad sight of the chief mourner, sitting alone in his carriage behind the coffin, amazed onlookers and made the children cry. For the chief mourner, a black ruff around his neck, was Tom Sayers' dog!

Like many other famous and successful people, Tom Sayers chose to be buried in the fashionable cemetery in Highgate. It had been opened about twenty-five years earlier when churchyards became too full to provide graves for the 50,000 Londoners who died every year. So Parliament agreed to a new idea—that seven cemeteries should be opened around London. Highgate Cemetery, high above the city, had splendid views of St. Paul's Cathedral and the Thames River winding away in the distance.

Tom Sayers' funeral procession, with his favorite dog, pony, and friends

Tom Sayers' dog, as it can still be seen today, lying on his tomb

18 The Dead Around Us

Arlington National Cemetery, where Americans who died in the two world wars and the Vietnam War are remembered. Here, too, many American presidents are buried. There is always a marine on guard.

Most big cities now have cemeteries—some are world famous, like Forest Lawn in California or Arlington National Cemetery near Washington, D.C.

All around us there are reminders of people who lived before us. A time detective can start to find out about people who lived nearby in the past from the names on war memorials, gravestones, and statues. Can you find names of families who still live locally?

You might be able to visit a site where archeologists are excavating a burial ground. Ask at your local museum.

It is unlikely that you will discover a tomb under the soil of your garden, but you may well dig up pieces of broken china or pottery, or the stem of an old clay pipe, or an old glass bottle. These remains were once objects used by people in their daily lives. Perhaps a farm worker enjoyed smoking the pipe after a hard day's work in the fields where modern houses now stand. Keep your eyes open—all around you there are clues to keep you busy as a time detective.

Glossary

adz ax with blade at right angles to the handle

Ancient Greeks the people who lived in Greece in the first few centuries B.C. and A.D.

archeologist a person who studies early human history, often by finding and examining remains and ruins

atlatl throwing stick used as a weapon

cairn heap of stones erected as a memorial

cemetery graveyard, from Greek word meaning "sleeping room"

columbaria word meaning "dovecote" in Latin, the Roman language. Roman tombs called columbaria had little holes to contain urns filled with the ashes of cremated bodies.

cremate to burn a dead body until it turns to ash

Egyptians a people who established an advanced civilization in Egypt from 4000 B.C.

embalm to prevent a dead body from decaying by treating it with chemicals or sweet-smelling oils

ibis bird like the stork, found in hot, wet areas

Inuit Eskimo people who live in Greenland

jet hard, black stone that shines when polished

ka ancient Egyptian word for a dead person's spirit, which could return to the mummified body after death and give it life

mastaba ancient Egyptian tomb with flat sides and sloping roof

mausoleum magnificent tomb, named after the tomb of the Greek king Mausolus

mica small glittering scales found in granite rock

mummy a dead body preserved and bandaged according to ancient Egyptian practice, to prevent its decay

neolithic later stone age, when people used polished stone tools and weapons

obsidian black glass from volcanoes

onager animal of the horse family, like a wild ass

Osiris ancient Egyptian god of the Underworld

pharaoh king of Ancient Egypt. The word meant "The Great House," for the Egyptians thought it rude to refer directly to their king, as they believed that he was a god.

prehistoric the time before there were written records

ritual a ceremony carried out according to strict rules

Romans a people from Italy who once ruled much of Europe

sarcophagus stone coffin, from the Greek word meaning "eater of flesh" because limestone coffins dissolved flesh

scarab ancient Egyptian jewel cut in the form of a beetle, with magic symbols on it

semiprecious stones jewel stones such as blue lapis lazuli or red garnet, which are less rare than precious stones—diamonds, rubies, sapphires, and emeralds

Sphinx stone lion with a human head which guards the pyramids at Giza. The head may be a portrait of Pharaoh Khafre. The Sphinx was one form of the sun god.

squash a large fleshy vegetable, the skin of which can be dried and used as a container

ushabtis small model figures of workmen placed in tombs in Ancient Egypt

vulture bird of prey

Index